GULITH

The Love Song Of Lancelot Biggs

Nelson S. Bond

ISBN: 978-1-63652-301-9

THE LOVE SONG OF LANCELOT BIGGS

NELSON S. BOND

Well, it's just like I told you. The last time you friends, dopes, and country hicks lent me your ears I said the *Saturn* was scheduled for an ordinary, routine, commonplace cargo shuttle to Uranus. But I also hunched it that inasmuch as my screwball pal, Lt. Lancelot Biggs, was treading the bridge almost anything was rather more than likely to happen.

And I was right. Only even in my wildest nightmares I didn't have any idea what was going to be chucked at us when we laid our lumbering old space-freighter down in the cradle at Sun City spaceport.

You see, the *Saturn* shuttles back and forth between the planets of the solar system, carrying everything and anything. When you carry cargoes like that, you often find yourself loaded up with plenty of trouble, and I don't mean maybe! And with Lancelot Biggs, those cargoes can *do* things!

What happened was that Johnston—he's the Interplanetary Corporation's port clearance official on Mars—came loping over to our jalopy like a hound in a hamburg orchard and closeted himself with Cap Hanson. For about a half hour they held privy council, as clubby as moths in an all-wool suit, and when they appeared again, the hush-hush was so loud it almost deafened you.

A few minutes later, stevedores started hauling into the *Saturn's* cargo bins an accumulation of air-tight, leaden containers. These workmen, too, were furtive as clergymen at a crap game, and all I could get out of them by way of explanation was the one word sentence, "Idunnonothinaboutit!"

So I hunted up Lancelot Biggs, who generally knows practically everything about practically everything, and of course I found him standing with one gangling arm draped limply about the shoulders of his brand-new bride, Diane Biggs (*née* Hanson), staring at a perfectly commonplace Martian sunset as though it were a gala world premiere presented especially for his benefit. And I complained, "Hey, Biggs! What's all the mystery about? What makes with the cargo?"

Biggs said, "Oh, hello, Sparks. Gorgeous evening, isn't it? You know, this magnificent sunset makes me think of that beautiful old Martian poem: '*To be with one's love when the scarlet orb....*'"

"Yeah," I said. "It's pretty, but unimportant. What I want to know is, who's hiding what from who? And if we're toting high explosives to Uranus, why doesn't the Old Man tell me so I can quit *now*?"

That got him. He snapped out of his trance and stared at me bewilderedly, his oversized Adam's-apple bobbing up and down in his throat like an unswallowed electric light bulb.

"What's that, Sparks? High explosives!"

And Diane said, "But that's impossible, Lancelot, dear. You *know* Daddy would have told us, if—"

That's as far as she got with her iffing, for at that moment the skipper himself came waddling across the field like a pint-sized tornado on toes and rasped, "All right, let's get going! Everybody aboard! Sparks, audio all hands to rocket posts and get your clearance O.Q. Lancelot, set trajectory for Iapetus—and make it snappy! We're lifting gravs immediately, if not sooner."

"*Iapetus!*" gasped Diane. "But—but, Daddy, I thought we were shuttling a cargo to Uranus?"

"*Was!*" snapped the Old Man. "Not is. Orders have been changed. Get going, everybody!"

Well, there are limits. I planted my tootsies in good old terra firma and said stubbornly, "Not me, Skipper. I'm not stirring a step till I know what this is all about. Why this sudden shift of destination?

And what were you and Johnston sneaking around corners to whisper about? And what are those lead cubes the cradle monks have been storing in our bin?"

"I ain't got time to explain now," said the Old Man. "Every minute counts. Now run along and—"

"Ah-hah!" I ah-hahed. "So it is explosives! O.Q., Skipper, consider me an ex-member of the *Saturn's* crew, as of two minutes ago. Space travel's dangerous enough without lousing it up with dynamite which might or might not. My aim is to sail the spaceways in *peace* ... not in *pieces*."

Cap Hanson's beefy face mottled dangerously, and he choked, "Confound you, Sparks, if there was another bug-pounder available I'd accept your resignation with whoops of glee. But as it is—Well, I'll tell you this much. It ain't explosives. It's something perfectly harmless but very valuable, which it's important we get to Iapetus before the Cosmic Corporation beats us there. *Now*—will you get goin', or do I have to—?"

"Oh, goody!" squealed Diane. "A race, eh, Daddy?"

"That's right," growled Hanson. "And a mighty important one, too, with about a quarter of a million credits hanging on it."

I sniffed. "Is that all? Then what's all the rush about? The race is not always to the swift."

"Oh, no?" The Skipper glared at me. "Says who?"

"Says a guy named Aesop."

"Well," snorted the Old Man, "all I got to say is that there Ee-sop friend of your'n didn't never bet on the ponies. Now, get goin', everybody, before I—"

So we went.

So we went, and of course with Lancelot Biggs on the bridge handling things it didn't take long to get going. Within a half hour we'd lifted gravs from Sun City, and in three shakes of a rocket's tail, Biggs had twisted our crate's nose about and pointed it at Saturn's eighth satellite, approximately 800,000,000 miles away.

Which left me with nothing to do till Slops gonged the dinner bell, so I was just sitting there reading the latest edition of *Spaceways Weekly* when the door of my turret opened and in walked L. Biggs.

Well, call it "walked" if you want to. That overworked verb neither accurately nor truthfully describes Lanse Biggs' peculiar style of locomotion. His method of self-propulsion is a sort of cross between a sidle and a galumph. Think of a giraffe wading in oiled ball-bearings, or a Mexican jumping-bean on stalks, and you'll have some idea what I mean.

Anyhow, he came in, closed the door behind him and grinned at me triumphantly.

"Well, Sparks," he chortled, "I found out!"

"Yeah?" I snorted. "Well, now if you mosey around and find *in*, too, you'll have both sides of the swinging door, won't you? Found out what? What are you talking about?"

"Why, what you wanted to know. I found out what we're carrying to Iapetus."

My interest revived like a zombie at a Black Mass. "You did?" I exclaimed. "Finally wormed it out of the Old Man, eh? Well—what is it?"

"Seeds," said Lance.

"Huh?"

"Seeds."

I said, "Don't look now, but there must be something wrong with my ears. It keeps sounding like you're saying 'seeds'."

"That's exactly," said Biggs patiently, "what I *am* saying, Sparks. We're carrying *seeds* to Iapetus. You know, little round—"

"Doogummies," I finished for him, "with unfledged thingamajiggers in 'em. Yeah, I know what seeds are. But I'll be damned if I know why we're carrying seeds almost a billion miles across space to a hunk of rock so cold and bleak that you have to thaw out the air before you can breathe it."

"That's just it!" explained Biggs excitedly. "You see, until just recently it was thought that the climatic conditions on Iapetus made that world uninhabitable. But recently an exploration party has discovered that after you melt your way through a quarter mile sheathing of ice, the entire planet is honeycombed with a vast, connected, sponge-like series of caverns. Good, warm, habitable caverns with earth to grow things in, and—"

"Ice to cold storage them in," I concluded, "after you've grown 'em. It sounds enticing—in a horrible sort of way. So who wants to live there? Snowmen?"

Biggs said soberly, "Practically everybody who's heard about the discovery. You see, Sparks, they not only learned that Iapetus could sustain human life; they also discovered that the entire planet is one great storehouse of precious mineral ores.

"Miners, adventurers, homesteaders ... humans from all over the solar system are flocking there as fast as they can drive their space-craft. Iapetus is a boom planet. It's a gold rush that makes Sutter's Mill and the Klondike seem like a polite game of musical chairs."

I moaned feebly and pawed what by this time ought to be—even if it ain't—my graying thatch.

"What you're saying," I complained, "begins not to make sense faster than ever. Thousands of people flocking to the Iapetus mines with picks and shovels and dreams of wealth ... and we join the gold rush with a cargo of seeds. Why?"

"But, don't you see?" explained Biggs. "Where there are mines there are humans. Where there are humans there are communities. Where there are communities—"

"People get hungry!" I burst in. "Of course! Now I get it. We're bringing them the seeds to sow vegetables with, is that it? And—oboyoboy! If we get there first, it'll be worth millions."

Because I had remembered the "most favored company" clause in the General Space Regulations, the paragraph which grants an eleven year commercial monopoly on any product to that company which first introduces any product to a newly-developed outpost of civilization.

These extra-territorial rights are the prizes for which outfits like ours and the Cosmic Corporation vie eagerly, because when you gain such a privilege it's just like finding a free pass to an eleven year ride on the gravy train.

One of the lushest feathers on our company's commercial cap is the monopoly on electric refrigerators to the Mercurian outpost, just as the deepest lines were graven on the face of our Board of Directors when the Cosmic Corporation grabbed the atmosphere-conditioning privileges on methane-blanketed Uranus.

But my glee was shortlived, for Biggs looked embarrassed. He shuffled from one foot to another like a cow in a quagmire. And—

"It's—er—they're not vegetable seeds, Sparks," he said meekly.

"Huh?" I gasped. "Then what *are* they? What other kinds of—?"

"Why—er—" said Lance, "they're flower seeds."

I said, "Flower seeds! Sweet howling serpents of Sirius! Curl my hair and call me a chrysanthemum! Has the whole darned I.P.S. gone lah-dee-dah? Why in the name of—"

Biggs said soberly, "Now don't get upset, Sparks. It's not so silly as it sounds. As a matter of fact, it's one of the most intelligent moves I've ever known the stuffed sh—I mean, the officials of our company to make. You see, flower seeds are a great deal more valuable than vegetable seeds."

"Oh, yeah! Sure! That's easy to prove, too. When a man's starving, just give him his choice between a loaf of bread and an orchid corsage—"

"No, Sparks, that's not the situation at all. You see, the problem here is not one of feeding the Iapetan colonists. They have plenty to eat. The satellite is so near its mother planet that edible supplies can be imported in great quantities. And even though food concentrates are not always particularly tempting to the palate—"

"Like," I told him, "dead fish ain't always particularly pleasing to the nostrils—"

"Nevertheless," continued Lancelot Biggs, "the Iapetan miners will have plenty of food. But to borrow an expression from a wise old book, 'Man does not live by bread alone.' There is such a thing, you know, as maintaining public morale, and one of the best ways of doing this is to offer people some small but tender fragment of beauty. Something to delight the eye with its color, soften the air with its fragrance. In short—flowers.

"You know, it's like some old Indian philosopher said way back in the 20th Century: If a man has but two coins in his pocket, he should take one of them and buy 'hyacinths wherewith to feed the soul'."

"Nevertheless—" I interrupted doggedly.

"So," pursued Biggs, "our company is being very clever in

hurrying this shipment of flower seeds to Iapetus. Not only because the people will love them, buy them, plant them eagerly for the pure, sensual pleasure of watching something grow—but also because there is big money in it.

"Didn't you ever hear of the famous Holland Tulip Market where fabulous prices were paid for unusual buds?[1] Who knows but that something like that might happen on Iapetus, and our company might make millions!"

"Out of which," I conceded grudgingly, "we might even collect a half day's pay as bonus. Well, maybe you've got something there, Lance. Maybe it *is* a good idea. But when I signed up for space service I never thought I'd end up as flower boy to a cosmic wedding."

This last comment elicited an unexpected result. At the word "wedding," Biggs stiffened like the feature attraction at a post-mortem. A frenzied look glazed his eyes.

"Oh!" he gulped. "Wedding! Sparks, thanks a million. I had almost forgotten."

"Forgotten what?" I demanded.

"Why, my anniversary."

"Anniversary! Are you off your beam? Why, you and Diane have only been married—"

"Two months," nodded Lancelot Biggs. "Day after tomorrow is our third anniversary." He swallowed sort of shyly, which is hard to do when your emotion exhibits itself in the frenzied leaping of a laryngial elevator. "Diane and I—well, we celebrate our wedding every month on the anniversary of the day we were married."

"And no quicker road to the poor-house," I sniffed, "was ever macadamized. So what are you going to do by way of celebration, Romeo? Take her to the observation deck and treat her to a view of the starry firmament revolving in its courses? That's about all the excitement there is available on this crate."

Biggs had been thinking furiously, a process which is always demonstrated by the way he shuffles from one foot to another. Now he snapped his fingers.

"No—I've got it, Sparks. Something unusual. A real surprise. Something that will startle and delight her."

"I know," I hazarded. "A new frock. You're going to whip it up in your spare time out of tarpaulin and old tablecloths."

"No, Sparks, I'm going to give Diane—" He paused dramatically—"flowers. Fresh flowers!"

I stared at him stupidly. And no cracks about how I couldn't very well do anything else.

"Flowers?" I repeated. "But where in blazes are you going to get fresh flowers out here in the middle of space?"

Biggs jerked a knuckly thumb in the general direction of the ship's hold. "Why, down there, of course. From our cargo bin."

I stared at him disgustedly. "Oh, sure," I drawled. "Pardon me all to hell. I plumb forgot about them. But look: aren't you overlooking one tiny detail? Those blossoms are in what is technically known as the 'papoose' stage. Which means they're only about six weeks shy of blooming. Not to mention the fact that at present they're planted in air-tight lead containers."

Biggs shrugged easily. "Oh, *that!*" he scoffed. "A mere nothing. Haven't you ever heard of hydroponic culture, Sparks?"

"Hydro-whichic-whature?"

"Hydroponic culture," he repeated. "It's a method of growing plants artificially in tanks of water chemically treated with the constituents necessary to growth. It's very old. Over three hundred years."

"Maybe so," I granted. "But those seeds are very young. And you've only got seventy-two hours to work in. Even with artificial culture, how are you going to bring them to full bloom in three days?"

Biggs said happily, "That's the most wonderful part of it, Sparks. It so happens that only recently I have been conducting a series of experiments on plant culture. If my theories are right, I think I have discovered a way to speed up the growth of living vegetation tremendously. Of course, my ideas are still only in the experimental stage, but I'm practically certain they will work."

I said, "Oh-oh!" and started for the door.

Biggs stared at me anxiously. "What's the matter, Sparks? Where are you going?"

"I don't know," I told him, "but wherever it is, it's a long way from here. I've had experience with inventions of yours before.[2] If you're going to start fiddling around again with things you don't know anything about—"

"But I *do* know *all* about it, Sparks," wailed Lancelot. "And I'm almost positive my plan will work. Now, be a good fellow, will you? Help me carry one of those lead containers up to that spare chamber on A Deck, and, let's see—I'll need a tank, a quart of vitamin B extract, an ultraviolet ray lamp—"

So, you know me. Lollypop Donovan, the eternal sucker. I helped him.

By way of alibi, I might as well confess here and now that I didn't think anything would come of Biggs' experiment. Oh, I know that in the past he has pulled so many bunnies out of the *chapeau* that his hat resembles a rabbit-warren. But this time I would have bet my somewhat battered immortal soul to the Black Gentleman with the Long Tail that Biggs had bitten off more than he could chew. 'Cause according to what my mama done tole me about the bees and the birds and the flowers, that biological phenomenon known as "life" requires a certain amount of time to establish itself.

But small items like impossibilities don't faze Mr. Biggs. He's the kind of a guy who never says die until he finds himself reporting for duty to the white-winged watchman at the Pearly Gates.

So for several hours he fiddled and diddled around with the complex array of gadgets he had accumulated, and finally he turned to me and said, with a smile of satisfaction, "Well, Sparks, there it is! How does it look?"

"It looks," I told him frankly, "like a nauseous bathtub on stilts. You mean you really expect to grow flowers in that overgrown fishbowl?"

"That's the idea."

"Well, how about the ultraviolet ray lamp? What's *that* for?"

"Why," said Biggs, "that's an important part of my new invention. It isn't ... er ... exactly an ultraviolet ray lamp any more, Sparks. I made a few minor adjustments on it. It now emits rays in the Hertzian range. That is, between one M and one-tenth CM in length, electrical waves for which—up till the present time—no use has ever been found. But if my theory is correct, they should irradiate the growing seeds pods with—"

"Never mind," I interrupted him hastily. "You're just wasting your breath and my time. Let's turn on the juice and see what happens."

"All right," said Biggs. "Let's have that container. What have we here anyhow? Ah! *Rosa rugosa!* They should be lovely. Diane will be delighted."

"Oh, hell!" I said. "Did we get the wrong container? Wait a minute. I'll go get one with flower seeds in it."

"No, Sparks. *Rosa rugosa* is a type of beautiful red rose. These should be exquisite. Here, I've got the seals open. Help me scatter some of these seeds carefully on the surface of the water ... there ... that's it! Now, the radiation—"

He clicked a switch and the lamp turned on. That is, I suppose it turned on. I wouldn't know about that exactly, for it emitted no light. But it must have been emitting *something*, for it did funny things to the light already existing in the room. It turned things all topsy-turvy.

You know how it is when you stand in front of a photographer's shop where they have those violet incandescents? Your flesh sort of turns bilious green and your lips look like something the cat dragged out of the well? Well, that's what happened now. I looked at Biggs and grinned, and he looked at me and split lavender lips in a blue-fanged, terrifying smile.

"Well!" he said. "There we are. Seventy-two hours from now, when we reach Iapetus, Diane should have a magnificent bouquet of dewy-fresh Earth roses, the first ever to be worn on that outpost."

"And seventy-two *seconds* from now," I told him, "I'm going to have the screaming meemies from looking at that grass-colored pan of yours. Let's get out of here."

Well, for the next couple of days nothing much happened. The *Saturn* had been cut over to the V-I unit,[3] of course, and we were jogging along at a very tidy and comfortable rate of 185,000 m.p.h. toward our destination. Having helped Lancelot Biggs to the best of my abilities, I now co-operated in his further efforts (to the betterment of my sanity) by remaining away from his experimental chamber. He, too, remained pretty much in seclusion. The only time I saw him was on the second day after noon mess when he came wandering up to my turret mumbling to himself like a cow in a clover path.

"Sparks," he demanded, "what rhymes with void?"

"Boid," I told him promptly. "Which I ain't ... and 'annoyed' which I am. Can't a hard-working radioman even catch up his slumbers around here without you getting in his hair? Why? When did you develop the poet complex?"

He flushed and laughed awkwardly, "Well, it—er—doesn't really matter," he temporized. "I was just trying to—Well, I thought it would be amusing to write a little poem to say to Diane when I gave her the roses. You know, a sort of a—love song."

"Some people," I snorted, "are born for trouble, and some people have trouble thrust upon them ... but you're the first guy I ever knew who went out of his way looking for it. Now it's love songs to go with the roses. By the way, how are the roses coming along?"

"Why, all right, I suppose," said Biggs. "I haven't been in to see them since yesterday. You see, I have the thermoes turned up to max in that room and it's pretty hot—"

"Not half so hot," I told him, "as the Old Man's going to be when he finds out you're the one who swiped that container from the cargo bin."

Biggs looked started. "Oh! Has he discovered one of them's gone?"

"You're darn tootin' he has! He came busting up here and asked me if I knew anything about it. I suggested maybe it was mice, but that didn't go over so big on account of mice don't generally build lead-covered bungalows. So if he happens to ask you, you'd better—"

"Better," interrupted an irate voice from the doorway, "what?"

The two of us spun like drunks in a revolving door. It was Cap Hanson himself, big as life and twice as furious. Biggs gulped.

"Oh—er—hello, Skipper. Sparks and I were just talking about—er—"

"About poetry," I finished. "Lanse was looking for a rhyme for—"

"Don't lie to me," blazed the skipper. "I heard what you was talkin' about. *So*, Lancelot! It was *you* tooken that container of seeds out of the cargo!"

Biggs said, "Why, yes, Captain, but—"

The Old Man suddenly remembered he was Lancelot Biggs' father-in-law as well as his chief. His face wrinkled like a prune, and he said in a melancholy voice, "Now, son, you shouldn't ought to have done that. Don't you know you're goin' to get in a peck of trouble? Them seeds was valuable."

"I know," replied Biggs, "but I just took a few seeds out of one of the containers. Nobody will ever notice. And—and it was our anniversary, you know. Diane's and mine."

The Old Man shook his head sadly.

"Lancelot, I'm surprised at you. Just took a few out of one of the containers? Don't you realize that whole box of seeds is ruined now? Why do you think they sealed them things in lead?"

Oh-oh! Suddenly, but belatedly, I knew what he meant. So did Biggs. The two of us stared at Hanson, then at each other haggardly.

Lancelot whispered, "Cosmic rays? Oh, my gracious! I forgot all about—"

"Sure, cosmic rays," groaned the Old Man. "You know they create mutants in dormant germinating cells. Now that them seeds been exposed they ain't worth a tinker's dam to anybody. They won't breed true. Lord only knows what kind of freaks and fiddle-di-diddles'll come up—if anything comes up at all." And he shook his head. "Lancelot, son, I'm sorry. But you know what I'm goin' to have to do. I'm goin' to have to enter this on the ship's log, and—and I'm afraid them seeds may cost you your job!"

It was just at that moment the *vocoder* on my set began chattering. The interruption suited me fine. I leaped to the controls and hastily tuned in my caller. But whatever pleasure I had felt dissipated instantly when I learned who he was and what he wanted. It was Tommy Jenkins, the bug-pounder at Ganymede IV, space-calling in Compang code.

He asked, "That you, Donovan?"

"It's not my grandmother," I retorted. "Why the Code, Tommy? What's up?"

"Taxes," said Jenkins, "skirt-lengths, and the Big Chief's blood pressure. Sparks, how far are you from Iapetus?"

I checked traj swiftly on my flight record. "About fifteen hours," I answered. "Twelve, maybe. Why?"

"Well, you'd better make it ten. Because we just got word the Cosmic Corporation freighter *Gemini* is closing in on Yappy with exactly the same thing you're carrying—a cargo of flower seeds! Orders are to beat them there at all costs. That is all. *Salujo!*" And he signed off.

I turned to the Old Man. "You heard that, Skipper?"

His face was the color of a 'dobe hut.

"I heard it," he croaked feebly, and stared at Biggs with lacklustre eyes. "Trouble, trouble; nothin' but trouble! Lanse, is there anything we can do to speed up a little?"

Biggs shook his head. "No," he groaned. "We're spinning the V-I unit almost at maximum acceleration now—185,000 plus. If we boost it any higher we're taking chances. We may exceed the limiting velocity of light and lose ourselves in the negative universe like we did once before." A sudden anger disturbed his usual calm complacency. "If we lose this race," he stormed, "the Company has nobody to blame but itself! *They* merchandised the V-I unit and made it available to every ship in space. Still—we must beat the C.C. to Iapetus, even if we have to take chances."

He turned to me suddenly. "Sparks, call Jenkins again. See if you can get an exact locus on the *Gemini*."

I did so. A few minutes later Biggs was seated at my plot table, anxiously scanning the course trajectories of both their ship and ours, reeling off involved and typically Biggsian mathematics that would have warped the gears of a calculating machine. The creases on his brow etched deeper as his columns of figures grew longer. Finally he stopped scribbling, lifted his head.

"Well?" asked the Old Man with bated breath. "What's the answer, son?"

"It's close," Biggs told us. "Perilously close. As near as I can figure, it's a nip and tuck race. They started later than we did, but their point of departure was nearer our mutual goal. From the viewpoint of distance alone, they should drop gravs on Iapetus one hour before we do."

Hanson groaned. "Licked again!"

"No," said Biggs. "Not quite. There's one thing which may save us. Iapetus' diurnal revolution. It's not simply a matter of *reaching* the satellite. They must actually beat us to the mining city. If their calculators have figured *our* position as we have figured *theirs*, they may be overconfident and think they've licked us just because they have an hour's advantage. And—this is risky, Cap, but—"

"Go on!" said the Old Man with rising excitement. Risks don't scare him. Danger is his bread and butter. "Go on!"

"If we can hold the velocity-intensifier in operation until just before we effect landing, we'll drop to normal acceleration right smack over that sector of Iapetus where the mines are, thus cancelling the sixty-odd minutes of stratosphere cruise the *Gemini* will have to make—and dropping us into the cradles at practically the same moment."

"If that happens," I broke in, "who gets the contract, Cap? Is there any provision for deadlock in the Space Regulations?"

The Skipper fumbled with the loose-leaf pages of his memory.

"Yeah," he finally decided, "there is. The Interplanetary Commerce Code rules that whenever two companies effect a simultaneous landing, their product shall be offered the governing board of the newly opened territory in direct competition."

I snorted loudly. "A hell of a lot of good that does us! It'll be a matter of choosing seeds against seeds. And if I know those Cosmic Corporation crooks, they'll bribe the Iapetus governing board blue in the face."

"Wait!" cried Biggs. "It may not be seeds against seeds. It may be seeds against—flowers!"

"Huh!" gasped the Old Man. "What was that, boy?"

"My ... er ... horticultural experiment," said Lancelot. "By the time we arrive there—perhaps by *now*—we may actually have flowers to show them. Exhibit A of the sort of thing our seeds will produce. It should provide a clinching argument."

Hanson stared at him bewilderedly. "You mean them seeds you swiped are growing flowers in three days?"

"That's what I hope," nodded Biggs. "Let's find out. Come down to my growth chamber and we'll see."

We needed no second invitation. In minus zero seconds the three of us were galloping down the ramp to the room wherein Lancelot Biggs had installed his hydroponic tank. We waited breathlessly as he fumbled with the lock ... then gasped and choked as the door opened and a steamy mist gushed out to smack us in the pans with an almost ponderable force. Then regardless of the heat the three of us were crowding into the narrow cubicle and—

A welter of tropic growths tumbled out of the door.

"Great snakes!" I gasped.

"Good goddlemitey!" croaked Cap Hanson.

"Oh, my gracious!" bleated Biggs.

For we had stepped not into the metal chamber of a space-craft bunkroom—but into what seemed the foetid fen of some steamy swampland jungle!

It's hard to describe what that room looked like. Imagine a Gauguin painting come to life ... a tropical hothouse gone berserk. That gives you some idea.

The original tank wherein Biggs had sprinkled the rose seeds was completely invisible, submerged beneath a crawling octopus of greenery. Writhing fronds spewed from the container to twist in tumultuous entanglement beneath our feet ... up the walls ... across the ceiling. Twining and spiraling around every piece of furniture, every bracket, any support to which suckered tendrils could cling. A heady perfume thickened the air; perfume from monstrous growths that no more resembled a rose than *I* look like a wasteland Martian.

Cap Hanson had been right. The action of cosmic rays had done weird things to those original germ cells.[4] *Rosa rugosa* had—figuratively and literally—gone crazy with the heat waves. Here triple-headed roses with spiny petals reared themselves awkwardly out of thick spongy, palmate foliage ... there a pinkish, cactus-like rose-thing clung tenaciously to a table leg ... elsewhere gossamer-fine, lavender petals, propelled by stirring gusts of air, drifted lazily across the room toward us, dangling epiphytic roots.

It was a startling exhibition of Mama Nature gone nuts! Only in two respects did these fantastic creations resemble the roses from which they were mutant. Each variation had thorns—as we discovered painfully when we tried to walk amongst them—and all had some shade or tint or hue of the fundamental red rose whence they had sprung.

Cap Hanson groaned, "Oh, my golly, what a mess! Of all the—Hey, let me out of here! Whatever's goin' on, it's gettin' *us*, too! Your faces!"

Biggs cracked indigo lips in what was supposed to be a placating grin but looked more like a hungry pitcher-plant licking its chops. He said, "The color means nothing, Captain. It's just a matter of light refraction."

"Which doesn't alter the fact," I reminded him, "that the experiment's a flop, Lanse, old boy. I—I guess we might as well call it quits. Clean this mess up and throw it away. We can't show this stuff to the Iapetus board. They'd toss us out on our necks."

Biggs nodded dolefully. "I guess you're right, Sparks. This is a bitter disappointment. I did *so* want to surprise her."

"Her?" grunted Hanson. "The Board's made up of hims."

"I mean," wailed Biggs plaintively, "Diane. Now she won't get her anniversary corsage...."

So that was that. The Skipper went back to the bridge to give our second in command, Lieutenant Dick Todd, the necessary trajectory instructions, and I stuck around, sweating and swearing, to help Biggs clean up the aboriginal morass he had created with his experiment. It was tough going, too. Like I said before, those roses had thorns. By the time we got done, our fingers looked like First Prize in a needlework exhibit.

It was just as we were finishing and Biggs was draining the final rugose drops of fluid from his tank that he loosed a little yelp of excitement.

"Sparks!"

"Now what?" I asked. "If it's another experiment—"

"Look! This one bred true in spite of the cosmic rays." And with quivering fingers he held up for my inspection one tiny bud which had been nestling coyly in a corner of the tank. A small but perfectly formed, brilliantly scarlet rosebud!

Well, I guess it was the irony of it that got me. I stared at the poor, pathetic, bedraggled little thing for a minute, then I chuckled.

"Well, there's the love song you were looking for, Biggs."

"Eh? What's that?"

"When you give her that bud," I told him, "you can say to her,

'Roses are red, violets are blue; the rest went whacky, but this one grew'."

Biggs said defensively, "Well, anyhow, this proves my theory about growth stimulation was right. It may not work in open space, but it will work on a planet where there are atmosphere blankets against cosmic ray penetration. And Diane *will* get one rose."

And with painstaking care he transferred the bud to a glass of water. Poor little pitiful symbol of a noble experiment which flopped.

And that was all until ten hours later. It's a shame to gloss over the excitement of those next ten hours, but it was mostly technical stuff you Earth-lubbers wouldn't understand.

The main point is that, though as a botanist Lancelot Biggs may be a bum Burbank, as an astrogator he is in a class by himself. His computations proved correct to four decimal places. We held the *Saturn* on the V-I unit until we were so close to Iapetus that the permalloy walls of our space-freighter started humming with tropospheric pressure, then released to normal acceleration, and— *bingo!* There we were, smack-dab over the new and as yet unnamed mining town. Just as Biggs had predicted.

Our appearance out of seemingly thin air—you understand what I mean if you know how the velocity-intensifier works—not only created a sensation on Iapetus; it darned near created an accident in our little segment of atmosphere. For when we switched over we found ourselves not more than a quarter mile from the Cosmic Corporation's *Gemini*, which had been easing into Iapetus complacently unaware that *we* were within several thousand miles.

Instantly there was hectic excitement upon both ships. Landing rocket jets flared, grav clamps growled, and the two of us hurtled groundward like brickbats.

It was a photo finish. We nosed into one cradle just as they stern-jetted into a second. And just as Cap Hanson leaped from *our* airlock, the *Gemini's* skipper burst from theirs.

Hanson bawled, "IPS-freighter-*Saturn*-landing-with-a-cargo-of-flower-seeds—"

His competitor screamed, "CC-freighter-*Gemini*-claiming-priority-on—"

But neither of them got to first base. A representative of the Iapetus colonists came to each ship, and the messages they delivered were identical.

"The governing board has decided that landings were effected simultaneously. Consequently you will present all wares for decision in open competition. Please report immediately to the general offices."

So there we were, a few minutes later, standing in the council room of the Iapetus governing board; Cap Hanson, Lancelot Biggs, Diane, and myself, glaring angrily across the room at representatives from our competitor space-craft, the *Gemini. Gemini* means "twins," which in this case was right, because the glares Cap Hanson and Cap Murgatroyd were hurling at each other were Siamese.

The Iapetus governor, an Earthman named Larrabee—said quietly, "Gentlemen, welcome to our new colony. Now ... I believe you each carry cargoes on which you wish to claim commercial priorities for your respective companies? Will you be kind enough to declare the nature of these cargoes?"

"Mine," said Cap Hanson loudly, "is flower seeds." And scowled at Murgatroyd.

"Mine," said Murgatroyd loudly, "is flower seeds." And scowled at Cap Hanson.

The Iapetus governor stroked his jaw thoughtfully.

"This is a delicate situation, gentlemen. You both carry a cargo our colonists will receive eagerly. It may be rather difficult to decide which of you—but I must let you present your own cases. What types of flowers are you carrying?"

"Roses," declared Cap Hanson defiantly. "Eighteen varieties of roses, includin' the rare, perennial Venusian swamp-rose."

"I see. And you, Captain Murgatroyd?"

"Thirty-four separate and distinct varieties of flowering plants," declared our opponent triumphantly, "including roses, geraniums, nasturtiums, pinks ... practically everything, sir!"

"Ah, yes. That seems to be a point in your favor, Captain Murgatroyd. Now—the size of your cargoes—?"

"Five hundred lead-sealed ten-bushel containers," gloated Captain Murgatroyd.

"Very good. And you, Captain Hanson?"

"The IPS," snarled the Old Man, "don't go in for samples! When we carry a cargo, we carry a cargo. Twelve hundred lead-sealed ten-bushel containers, Your Honor!"

"Excellent! Excellent, Captain! That seems to be a point in *your* favor. This is most difficult. Er ... Captain Murgatroyd ... perhaps you could give us some idea as to the growth potentialities of your flowers?"

Murgatroyd grinned and dug into an inner pocket, brought forth a folder which he placed in the Governor's hands.

"Yes, sir. Here is a four-color brochure issued by our Company, describing each and every type of plant we have brought to Iapetus, and reproducing pictures of those flowers in full natural color."

The Governor shook out the papers, and my heart played tag with my shoestrings. The CC's publicity department had done a magnificent job. Those natural color photographs were luscious enough to make the mouth of the rankest amateur gardener water. Gay yellows and soft blues ... brilliant splotches of crimson ... dainty, sunny marigolds ... shy nodding violets ... that pamphlet was a tempting hunk of stuff.

But I had been wrong in thinking the Governor of Iapetus could be bribed. He was an honest man. He turned to Cap Hanson.

"And you, Captain? Have you a similar brochure?"

The Old Man scrubbed his jaw feebly. "Why ... er ... the truth is, Your Honor—" he began.

It was then Lancelot Biggs stepped forward, interrupting the skipper.

"The truth is, Governor," he said blandly, "*our* Company does not depend on printed booklets to sell its products. There is, you surely realize, a certain amount of artistic falsification—or should I simply call it 'artistic license'?—employed in reproducing facsimiles of living objects. Therefore, in order to sell *our* goods we always attempt to offer a living example of our product.

"I have here—" He dug into his jacket pocket and brought forth a bulging waxine envelope—"the bud of one of our most gorgeous blooms, the famous *Rosa rugosa*. You can see for yourself—"

With the look of a proud papa he opened the flap of the envelope, started to withdraw his single rosebud, and—stopped suddenly. A look of startled alarm drained his face of all color. He whispered, "But—but this—"

"Go on, lad," prodded the Old Man. "Show 'em. You got a bud there, ain't you? Well, show 'em."

But Biggs didn't show 'em. Instead, he closed the envelope

again, slipped it back into his coat pocket, and his liquescent larynx bobbled frantically as he said,

"I—I'm sorry, gentlemen. I haven't anything to show you."

"Why?" I demanded. "Lanse, for gosh sakes, *why*? What's happened to—"

He turned to me haggardly. "The bud—" he choked—"*died*!"

Well, I'll hand it to that Governor. He was not only honest; he was so fair and square you could have used him for a measuring rod. He said consolingly, "That's too bad, Mr. Biggs. But accidents will happen. Is there anything further you have to say on behalf of your product?"

"I got plenty to say!" stormed the Skipper. "Just on account of one bud died don't mean we ain't got—"

"Excuse me, Skipper," interrupted Lancelot Biggs mildly. "I—I think the time for deceit has passed."

"*What!* What's that?"

"I think the governor should be told the truth," said Biggs. "We should confess that our seeds are not a first class product. Might not, indeed, even flourish in the soil of Iapetus."

"Lanse!" I cried. "Do you know what you're saying? Don't talk like that!"

"Yes, Governor," nodded Lancelot Biggs sorrowfully, "I'm afraid that's true. Your colony wouldn't want our seeds. For one thing, they're all roses. The Cosmic Corporation offers you all kinds of flowers. For another thing, our seeds are not particularly hardy. Furthermore, I'm afraid a number of them were spoiled in transit when the leaden containers were broken, allowing cosmic rays to seep in—"

"*Biggs!*" howled Cap Hanson. "Shut up this minute an' get out of here! What do you mean by tellin' lies like that? A number of our containers? It was only *one* container, and—"

The Governor interrupted him with a smooth lift of the hand. "Never mind, Captain Hanson. We understand. Er ... thank you, Mr. Biggs, for your frank statement. Gentlemen of the Council, you have reached a decision? Yes, I thought so.

"Captain Murgatroyd, it gives me great pleasure to award you, on behalf of the Iapetus Governing Board, full priority rights to the flower-seed concession on our new colony, as set forth in Rule 14, Paragraph—"

"*Ruined!*" wailed Cap Hanson. "Sabotaged by a wolf in cheap clothing! Diane, why did you ever marry that falsifying, good for nothin'—"

He broke down. We led him, babbling incoherently, back to the ship.

But there, Diane, who had held up nobly throughout the proceedings, turned to her husband curiously.

"Lanse, dear, you know I've always backed you up in everything you've done, but—but why did you do this? Don't you know the loss of this monopoly will cost the Company millions, and may cost Daddy his job?"

Lanse nodded. "Yes, I know that would be true, dear ... if there were not other factors involved."

Cap Hanson lifted his head drearily.

"Other factors?"

"Yes, Skipper. Something amazing has happened. Something

so incredible that even yet I can scarcely credit it. It all turns about something Sparks said—"

"Who, me?" I gulped. "Now, don't drag *me* into this."

"You remember that ... er ... love song you suggested to me?" queried Biggs.

I nodded glumly. "Sure. '*Roses are red, violets are blue, the rest went whacky—*'"

"But this one—" finished Lancelot Biggs triumphantly—"is *blue*!"

And dramatically he drew from its waxine envelope the rosebud he had refused to show the Iapetus Governor, tossed it on the table before us. We all stared at it in gasping bewilderment. For he was right. That tiny rosebud was a brilliant, penetrating, heavenly, *cobalt blue*!

Cap Hanson choked, "But—but a blue rose! I never seen such a thing before!"

"Neither," crowed Biggs, "has anyone else. But flower-lovers have dreamed of them for centuries.[5] Hundreds of thousands of dollars—perhaps millions—have been spent by botanists in an effort to create that rare, often wished for but never accomplished example of beauty, the blue rose. A fortune awaits the first man to put such a thing on the market. And by luck we have done it!"

"You—you mean people will *buy* this thing?"

"From now," declared Biggs, "until the end of time! This single mutant will parent a whole new breed of blue roses, and botanists throughout the entire solar system will mortgage their hothouses to buy slips from this parent plant.

"Now you see why I couldn't show it to the governor, I couldn't risk letting the secret get out until we had taken the bud back to Earth, patented it in the name of the IPS.

"Incidentally—" He coughed delicately—"our Company should be very pleased. I think we may anticipate a considerable bonus for our part in creating this new species."

I said, "But, hey—wait a minute! There's something wrong somewhere. I seen that bud before. But when I did, it wasn't blue! It was as red as an old maid's face at a strip-tease!"

"*Looked* red, you mean," corrected Biggs. "Not *was* red. That was a matter of color reflection, Sparks, caused by the Hertzian ray lamp I had installed in the laboratory. You will remember our faces were green, our lips purplish. You see, color is a tricky thing. For instance, when you see a green leaf, what color is that leaf?"

"Why, you just said. Green, of course."

"Ah, no!" said Biggs. "It is *every color but green*! Colors by which we designate objects are *not* their true colors. Quite the reverse. They are the colors those objects reflect.[6] Under the Hertzian wave this precious bud—" He caressed it fondly—"apparently reflected all colors save red. We therefore thought it a normal red rose. But now that we see it under ordinary light, we realize it absorbs the red range as well as all others save the blue."

He shrugged. "So—there you are! And now, darling, if you will allow me, I would like to give you a little anniversary present. The first blue rose ever to be grown—"

But Cap Hanson snatched the bud from his hand feverishly.

"Oh, no, you don't! That there thing goes right back into your fish pond and keeps growin' until we get back to Earth. Which is goin' to be as quick as we can make it, or maybe more so. If you two gotta have an anniversary treat, I'll see to it that Slops whips up a special banquet tonight, complete with champagny-water an' everything. How's that?"

And from the look in Diane's and Lancelot's eyes as they moved toward each other, I guessed it would probably be all right. For when a man and a woman feel that way about each other, they don't really need special dates to celebrate.

Anyhow, Lancelot Biggs had warbled his song of love. "Love sends a little gift of roses." Yeah—*blue* roses! But what did you expect? That whacky wingding of the spaceways never does anything in a normal way.

Or—does he?

<hr>

[1] "Every reader possibly knows of the 'Tulip Mania' in Holland (1634 to about 1638 A.D.) when speculation in bulbs became as wild as speculation has been at other times on the Stock Market. A record price of 13,000 florins (equal to about 260,000 florins today, or $104,000 American money) is reported to have been paid during the mania for one bulb of the variety *Semper Augustus*." Gager: *The Plant World*.—ED.

[2] For stories of Sparks' experiences with Lancelot Biggs' inventions, see copies of *Fantastic Adventures* and *Amazing Stories*, 1940-1-2.—ED.

[3] The V-I (velocity-intensifier) unit is an invention of Lt. Lancelot Biggs which permits space-craft to attain velocities approaching the "limiting velocity" of light, i.e., approximately 186,000 miles per second.—ED.

[4] Science has already discovered that the bombardment of cosmic rays is at least partially responsible for the creation of "freaks," "sports," or "mutants," in both the animal and vegetable world. Life on atmosphere-blanketed planets is not subject to this bombardment, because of the protective Heaviside energy layer ... but space-craft must be carefully shielded from such radiation.—ED.

[5] "Although the attempt has often been made to produce a blue rose, no one has ever succeeded.... The reason a blue rose has never been produced is that blue has never arisen spontaneously in the Genus *Rosa*, and no blue flower of another genus has ever been found that will ... transfer its blue color to the latter. A breeder who could do this would ... make a fortune." Gager: *The Plant World*.—ED.

[6] "Sunlight, as Sir Isaac Newton discovered, is a combination of the seven colors that compose the spectrum. An object is red because it is so constituted that it reflects the red rays of a beam of sunlight but absorbs all others ... a lily is white because it reflects all the rays ... a buttercup is yellow because it reflects only the yellow rays, absorbing all others ... an object is black because it absorbs all the colors of the spectrum." Gager: *The Plant World*.—ED.

www.ingramcontent.com/pod-product-compliance
Lightning Source LLC
Chambersburg PA
CBHW071145250626
47159CB00006B/2305